MR.
CHATTERBOX

by Roger Hargreaves

WITHDRAWN

PSS!
PRICE STERN SLOAN

Mr. Chatterbox was one of those people who simply couldn't stop talking.

He used to talk to anybody and everybody about anything and everything, going on and on and on.

And on and on and on!

And on and on and on!

And when he didn't have anybody else to talk to,
he used to talk to himself.

"Good morning, Mr. Chatterbox," he used to
say to himself.

"Good morning to you," he used to reply to himself.

"Nice day, isn't it?"

"Yes it is, for this time of year."

And so on, and so on, and on and on!

He lived in a village in a box-shaped house:

Chatterbox Cottage!

One morning the mailman arrived with a letter for him.

"Morning, Mr. Chatterbox," said the mailman.

"Ah, good morning to you, Mailman," replied Mr. Chatterbox. "Although, as I was saying to myself only yesterday, or was it the day before? I forget, however, it's not quite so good a morning, in my opinion, but I might be wrong, although I'm not very often, as it was the other day, Monday I think it was, or perhaps it was Tuesday? But never mind, because it is quite a good morning, don't you agree? Yes of course you do, because that's what you said to me in the first place, and . . ."

And he went on and on all morning and the poor mailman was late delivering all his letters.

That afternoon Mr. Chatterbox went into the hat shop in the village.

"Hello, Mr. Bowler," he said to the man who owned the hat shop. "Do you think, if it's possible, that I could buy, if it's not too expensive, but I'm sure it won't be, a new hat? Because, would you believe it? Yes of course you would, but anyway, as I was saying, my present hat, the one on my head, as you can see, is getting, how can I put it? A little too old, because I've had it for, let me see now, it must be, let's think, ten years? No, I tell a lie, it can't be that long, or can it? Well, yes it could be, but on the other hand . . ."

And he went on and on all afternoon and half the night, long after poor Mr. Bowler should have closed the store and gone home.

Eventually, when Mr. Bowler managed to get a word in edgewise (or was it sideways?), he promised to order a new hat for Mr. Chatterbox.

Then he pushed Mr. Chatterbox—still talking of course—out of his shop, and went home for his supper—which was cold of course—because Mrs. Bowler had cooked it for him hours ago.

And, while he ate, Mr. Bowler thought.

Exactly one week later, the new hat for Mr. Chatterbox arrived in a snazzy red hatbox.

The mailman delivered it to Mr. Bowler's shop.

"At last," said Mr. Bowler, heaving a sigh of relief. "This hat is going to solve the problem of Mr. Chatterbox talking so much."

"I wish it could," said the mailman. "But how can it?"

"Because," replied Mr. Bowler, "this hat is a magic hat!"

"Oh," replied the mailman, who didn't quite understand.

That same afternoon Mr. Bowler took the new hat to Chatterbox Cottage.

"Oh, goody," said Mr. Chatterbox, grabbing the hat-box and opening it. "It's my new hat, my lovely new hat, I couldn't wait for it to arrive, in fact, I got up early this morning, because, aren't I silly? I just knew, I don't know how, but I really knew, you know, that today would be the day, I don't know how I knew, but I knew, and it is, and here's my hat, and oh, isn't it beautiful? I can't wait to try it on, oh I do hope it looks good on me, do you think it will? Yes of course you do, and—"

"Why don't you try it on," said Mr. Bowler, grinning.

"Try it on? Yes, of course I must try it on, how silly of me to stand here chattering away when I haven't tried it on yet, yes, I will, absolutely, definitely, try it on right away, because, as I said, it's silly just to talk about trying it on, and then not try it on, isn't it? And so . . . "

He took the hat out of the hatbox, and put it on.

It was a beautiful hat!

"I say," he said. "I must say, yes I really must, that this hat, is, yes it really is, to say the least, one of the better hats that I have ever seen in my life, and in my life, I must say, I have seen some hats, and furthermore . . ."

But while he was talking a funny thing was happening: The more Mr. Chatterbox talked, the more the hat grew and grew.

Mr. Chatterbox kept on talking and the hat kept on growing.

"I can't see anything," he said. "One minute I was standing here looking at my new hat in the mirror, and now, all of a sudden, without any warning, surprising me no end, just like that . . ."

The hat grew down to his feet, and Mr. Chatterbox stopped talking.

And as soon as he stopped talking, the hat grew smaller and smaller, until it was the same size as when he'd first tried it on.

Mr. Bowler had walked away while Mr. Chatterbox was under the hat and couldn't see him.

And now Mr. Bowler was walking to his shop.
"My special magic hat really works," he chuckled.

The following day, Mr. Chatterbox was out for a walk when he met the mailman in the village.

"Hello, Mailman," he said. "Hey, do you like my new hat? Have you ever seen such a fine hat? I'm sure you never have, what a hat, and . . ."

But you know what happened, don't you?

The hat grew and grew and grew the more Mr. Chatterbox talked.

"Now I know what Mr. Bowler meant by a magic hat," chuckled the mailman. And he went on his way, leaving poor Mr. Chatterbox speechless.

Hmm, Mr. Chatterbox thought, thinking.
Not talking—thinking!

And do you know something?

That hat taught Mr. Chatterbox his lesson.

And these days he doesn't talk half as much as he used to, or even a quarter as much. And you know the reason for that, don't you?

Yes, of course you do.

But . . .

. . . keep it under your hat!